The Magical, Marvelous Megan G. Beamer

A Day in the Life of a Dreamer

a grandma rose story

GR PUBLISHING
FELTON, CA

© 2004 by GR Publishing
Felton, CA 95018

Illustrations ©2003 Laurie Barrows

Cover design ©TLC Graphics, www.TLCGraphics.com

Burnett, Karen Gedig.
    The magical, marvelous Megan G. Beamer : a day in the
life of a dreamer / by Karen Gedig Burnett; illustrated
by Laurie Barrows.
    p. cm.
    SUMMARY; All day Megan runs, plays and acts out as
people tell her to stop it and grow up. Dejected, she turns
to her mother for comfort, love and support.
  Audience: Ages 5-10
  LCCN 2003094182
  ISBN: 09668530-5-9 (hardback)
  ISBN: 09668530-6-7 (softback)

  1. Individuality–Juvenile fiction. 2. Mother and
child–Juvenile fiction. [1. Individuality–Fiction.
2. Mother and child–Fiction.] I. Title.

PZ7.B93413Ma 2004   [E]
                      QB133-1434

10 9 8 7 6 5 4 3 2 1

Printed in Hong Kong

IN MEMORY OF

Matthew Ray Andersen
*Like Megan, your spirit soared.
Ride, Free Spirit, Ride!*

AND

Phyllis Ann Gedig
*A mother's love
lasts more than a life time.*

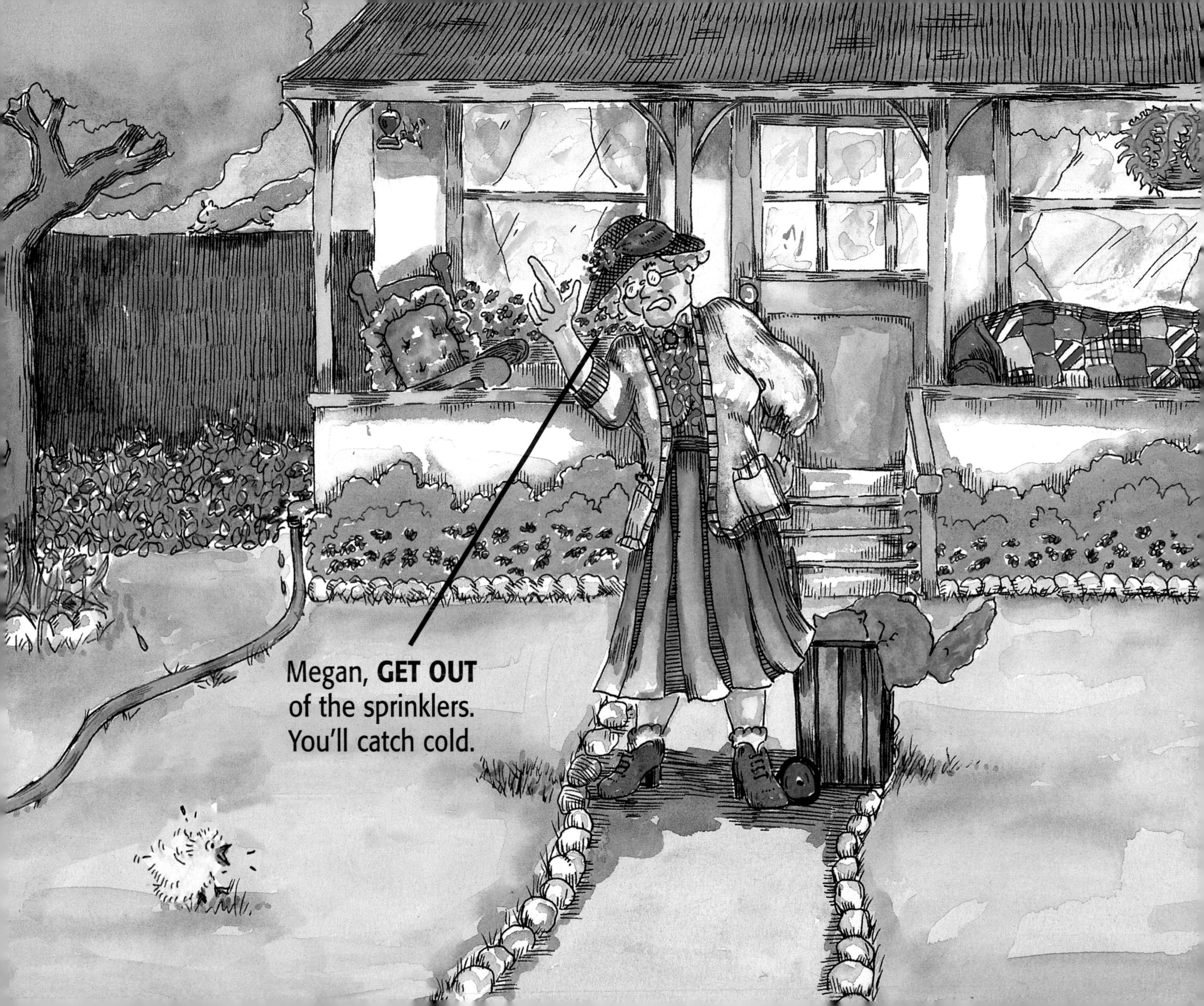
Megan, **GET OUT** of the sprinklers. You'll catch cold.

People keep saying,"Don't!"
"Stop!" "Grow up!" "Get lost!"

Why does everyone want me
to be different than I am?

But Megan, I love your dreams.
I love your energy.

And even though I get tired
sometimes and can get crabby,

I wouldn't change you.

I love you just the way you are.

Really?

Note to parents, grandparents, teachers, and all who love and care for children:

No! Stop! Don't! Get out! Grow up!

Let's face it, children make lots of mistakes. After all, they haven't lived as long or learned all the rules we, as adults, take for granted. Children are also more impulsive and haven't developed the ability to think things through yet. It's natural then, that as adults, we want to guide and teach our children, as well as protect them as they grow. However, sometimes our guidance falls short. Instead of enveloping them with gentleness and love as we explain things to them, we find ourselves ordering, criticizing or judging them harshly.

Children not only endure streams of judgment and criticism from us as adults, but also from older children as well. Surely, the more active, inquisitive, and independent a child is, the more that child is going to fail to meet someone's expectations, and therefore, bear the brunt of an angry person's disapproval. From a child's perspective, how must it feel to be the lowest one on the pecking order, to constantly be criticized, and therefore, get "pecked" at the most?

Negativity directed toward a child can have an impact on that child's self esteem. Children should not be allowed to do anything they want without regards to any consequences. Clearly, our guidance and support is needed in order for them to learn sensitivity toward others, to recognize and deal with their feelings, and to think before they act. However, in order to make the most positive and lasting impression on a child, our guidance needs to originate from love.

Love does not judge or criticize; it observes, explains, allows for natural consequences, and may even imposes logical consequences. Love sees the long-term importance rather than the short-term convenience. Love shows patience, understanding and acceptance.

Harold S. Hulbert once said, "Children need love, especially when they do not deserve it." Isn't that true for all of us?

Our children look to us to gain a sense of who they are. The more we shower them and ourselves with love, the more they will learn to love themselves. If we are willing to catch ourselves when we are about to judge or criticize, and instead, give our children the kind of love, gentleness and respect that we, too, would like to receive, our children will flourish beyond our wildest dreams.

Karen Gedig Burnett

Karen Gedig Burnett (a.k.a. Grandma Rose)

P.S. A wonderful book offering respectful and effective ways to deal with children is
Parenting With Respect and Peacefulness by Louise A. Dietzel.